'There is nothing more deceptive than an obvious fact.'

Sherlock Holmes,
in The Boscombe Valley Mystery

‘A library is thought in cold storage.’

Herbert Samuel (British politician, 1870 – 1963)

– so is a book, so enjoy thawing out the thoughts herein!

Never Odd or Even
by John Townsend

Published by Ransom Publishing Ltd.
Radley House, 8 St. Cross Road, Winchester, Hampshire SO23 9HX, UK
www.ransom.co.uk

ISBN 978 178127 102 5
First published in 2013

A CIP catalogue record of this book is available from the British Library.

BIO LEG SLOT

LOST BOG LIE

GET OIL SLOB

SOLO GIBLET

OBLIGE LOTS

BOGIES TOLL

LET BOILS GO

12

100

2

Can you keep a secret? I've never revealed the hidden truth before, but now I'm about to tell someone. You.

First of all, here's a clue about who I am – I'm at that special age: 12.

12 is one of my favourite numbers in the whole universe. In fact, it's my perfect number. 12 isn't just the sum of 10 (the base of our whole

amazing number system) and 2 (the only even prime number in the cosmos) but it's the first number with 1, 2, 3 and 4 as factors. I reckon that's so cool.

But it's not just numbers that are magic. Letters are my thing, too. People think I'm weird because I spend a lot of my time watching Countdown, playing Scrabble or doing Sudoku. They say that's really odd when you're 12. But I don't care. I always say I'm never odd or even.

You'll soon find out what I mean.

I don't know when it started. Probably as soon as I could talk. It's something inside my brain and that's all there is to it. If you don't like it, you just have to leave me alone.

That's what Mr Adam says. He reckons I'm a puzzle – which is cool because puzzles are my best thing of all. He said to me, 'Eliot, how can you solve a Rubik's Cube in seconds but never work out how to listen properly? You are an enigma!'

I, ENIGMA? IMAGINE!

I love anagrams like that. Anyway, I told Mr Adam I don't need to listen all the time because I just seem to know lots of stuff. He's

my form teacher, but he didn't understand because I spoke backwards.

That's something else I do.

The thing is, if I weren't good at puzzles, the police would never have solved the crime.

I actually sorted it out for them. Mr Adam said it showed that my odd brain shouldn't be seen as a problem but a **POUR IN POTTY**. (That's an anagram for **OPPORTUNITY**.)

He said I should write down what happened in a blog, to see if anyone else can solve the crime before I reveal a few hidden secrets. See if you can spot the clues and solve the biggest mystery that struck our school in the history of the world.

I'm going to tell you exactly what happened on the day a **BURGLAR STRUCK (GRUB CART LURKS**).

You see, I just can't help doing anagrams. That annoys a lot of people. Maybe I'm annoying you with my word puzzles – but I'll try hard not to upset you too much. **I PROMISE**. (**IRIS POEM** – oops, sorry.)

Before I tell you all about how I solved a crime for the police, I'm going to give you a

puzzle to solve. It was Mr Adam who got me started. He once said to our class, '**MADAM I'M ADAM**' and I knew what he meant straight away.

So in a few seconds I replied with '**WAS IT ELIOT'S TOILET I SAW?**'. How cool is that? That's the puzzle for you to solve. Get it?

Mr Adam had to explain to everyone else what *palindromes* are (which I immediately made into **PROMISE LAND, RANDOM SPIEL** or **ROMP IN DALES**).

I just love words and numbers that are the same backwards or forwards. That's why I've called my blog **NEVER ODD OR EVEN**.

(Or if you prefer anagrams: **REDDEN OVER OVEN, DODO NEVER NEVER, OVER END OVER END**.) Sometimes I even talk in anagrams just for fun.

So now you know my special hobby, here's my secret fact sheet. I call it Eliot's stuff.

Favourite band	**ABBA**
Favourite car	**A TOYOTA** (**RACECAR**)
Favourite machine	**ROTAVATOR**
Favourite invention	**RADAR**

Favourite time of day **NOON** (or **12.21**)

Best friends

ROBERT TREBOR

A LAD NAMED E. MANDALA

EVIL OLIVE

HANNAH (She's the only real person in the list)

Favourite place (in Alaska)

KANAKANAK

Favourite year **2002**

Favourite date **21.11.12**

Favourite word

AIBOHPHOBIA (fear of palindromes!)

I like to think a lot. After all, there's lots to think about when you're 12.

Each night before I go to sleep, I work out sums in my head and try to answer some big questions. Before I get on to my story, I'll give you my latest five big questions. I don't have all the answers yet.

1. What colour is Friday?

2. In how many ways could you be friends with your enemy?

3. What if the number 12 had never been invented?

4. What's the biggest number in the universe – if I add on 12?

5. Do geese see God? (This one is extra cool – but can you see why?)

Eliot's 5 science questions to keep me awake at night:

1. Where does the light go when you switch it off?

2. What are shadows made of?

3. Why is the Sun usually yellow? (Come to think of it, why are dusters yellow as well?)

4. Does the Sun make a noise? (Even if there's no one near enough to hear it.)

5. If you travel faster than light and shine a torch ahead of you:

a) would you see yourself coming back?

b) would the torch beam be travelling faster than light?

c) if you went through a black hole, would your torch still work, or would you need new batteries? (Maybe cadmium batteries, as cadmium has the atomic number 48 – a special Eliot Number!)

It happened last Friday – the perfect day for a crime. It was 12th July, which made it even more perfect. It was my duty day in the library. I'm a library prefect. In fact, I help in the library every lunchtime – for three special reasons:

1. Mrs Eve is the librarian and she's got a big biscuit tin that she calls her Chamber of Secrets. I have been entrusted as its

ANOINTED GUARDIAN. Or **A DEAD NUN A-RIOTING**.

2. Libraries are safe and full of amazing words.

3. Libraries use the Dewey Decimal System to keep everything in order. **PERFECT** for a **PREFECT**!

I like the 510 section in the library best, which is maths and numbers. But I've also read a lot of **HE'LL MOCK HORSES**. Can you guess that anagram? Those books are on the fiction shelves

(CL–CU) and they're great for people who like solving crime puzzles.

Do you know what I'm going on about? I'll tell you – **SHERLOCK HOLMES**. I really like detective stories, especially those written by Arthur Conan Doyle. Mrs Eve says I would make a good Sherlock Holmes because I'm always solving things. I like Mrs Eve for three special reasons:

1. Her name is a palindrome.

2. She is a perfect match for Mr Adam.

3. She lets me use her computer and sort out her software. I love computers.

Mrs Eve says I make her laugh a lot, which is weird because I don't really know any jokes. I don't even *like* jokes. She also said that my head must be a computer, which is also a bit weird because my head never needs to be plugged into the wall.

But even though Mrs Eve says odd things sometimes, I like it in the library. She says I keep it running like clockwork. I think she means that (the *clockwork* thing) because I'm 12 – so I'm the top library prefect, like the 12 at the top of a clock. Otherwise I don't see that a library is anything like a clock. Although I think some old libraries are round, like one I saw in a book on Oxford on the 941 shelf.

I told Mrs Eve that being a librarian is an ideal job for me. That's because an anagram of **LIBRARIAN** is **BRAIN LAIR**, which is exactly what a library is – a refuge and a place of hiding for my mind. Perfect. She just smiled.

I like Fridays. It's when I'm in charge of the library all lunchtime and I get to eat my sandwiches in Mrs Eve's office, next to her biscuit tin. I also like Fridays because:

1. I have Maths, English, Science and History on the same day – my best subjects.

2. I don't have *yuck* Citizenship, Drama, PE or Art.

3. We finish the afternoon with longer form time with Mr Adam, who gives me puzzles.

The reason why Friday was the best day for a burglary was because that's when the school office is left empty for twenty-five minutes. It's a window of opportunity for any thief.

Those twenty-five minutes are when Mrs Harris (she's a sort of money manager who wears pink cardigans, has a squeaky voice and giggles a lot) always attends the finance meeting with the headteacher and a couple of men in suits.

Her office is always left empty from 11.10 to 11.35 every Friday. I found this out on the day I got hit by a ball on the field at morning break and I had to sit in her office with a bag of frozen peas on my head. I heard Mrs Harris saying (mainly squeaking) lots of things that day. I also saw where the school safe is hidden.

There's a big splodgy painting on the wall behind Mrs Harris's desk that opens like a little door because it's fixed to the wall on hinges. Built into the wall behind it is a metal safe with an unusual lock.

Mrs Harris keeps the key in her handbag, but I think there must be a spare one somewhere, in case she's away.

Well, I got a peep inside that safe from the floor, when I had to lie down with the frozen peas. There was a lot of money in bundles, a cash box, a bag of £2 coins and a few silver cups and trophies.

Mrs Harris didn't see me peeping through my fingers. I saw her lock the safe door, put the painting back and drop the key in her purse inside her handbag. (I was disappointed it wasn't a combination lock using numbers. *That* would have been awesome.)

The phone rang and Mrs Harris giggled into it with a squeak:

'I'm just coming, Derek. Just attending to the walking wounded – although Eliot's not so much walking as lying on the floor with his feet up on a chair to get the colour back to his cheeks, bless him.'

She giggled again and said to me with a very loud voice (I think she thought I couldn't hear very well if I had a bag of peas on my head), 'I'll be back in a minute, poppet. I've just got to go to the finance meeting. Just call Miss Milligan in the next office if you need anything.'

Then off she went, and I was left lying there ... staring at the splodgy picture behind her desk and knowing that I must be one of the only pupils in the school who knew what was hidden behind it.

Before I tell you about something terrible and all about the **BIG KERFUFFLE (ELF BIKER GUFF)** that started the mystery, you might like to know about one of my special laws. I call them **ELIOT'S NUMBERS CRUNCH LAWS**.

I'll put it in a box in case you want to skip over it and miss it out. Mr Adam says I must try to think about other people who don't like numbers, because if I keep going on about them I might be boring.

So the next bit in the box (**ELIOT'S NUMBERS CRUNCH LAWS: LAW 1**) is for people who like numbers and who want to think *inside* the box. Mr Adam says I'm always thinking *outside* the box – but I don't really understand what that means.

If you like numbers, can you answer this question: What numbers are never odd or even?* There's an obvious answer. I've put it at the bottom of this page, upside-down.

Now, are you ready to look *inside* the box?

**Fractions. Fractions are never odd or even.*

ELIOT'S NUMBERS CRUNCH LAWS: LAW 1

Certain numbers with two digits are never odd or even.

Why? Some numbers from 10 to 99 are *both* odd and even.

PROOF: Choose any number between 10 and 19 … Example: 12. Odd or even?

Answer: **Even** (because it can be divided by 2).

BUT: add the two digits of 12 together:

1 + 2 = 3 (which is an odd number).

CONCLUSION: 12 can be both odd and even.

Choose any number between 90 and 99 …

Example: 99. Odd or even?

Answer: **Odd** (because it cannot be divided by 2).

BUT: add the two digits of 99 together:

9 + 9 = 18 (which is an even number).

CONCLUSION: 99 can be both odd and even.

This will work for every number between: 10 and 19, 30 and 39, 50 and 59, 70 and 79, 90 and 100.

But not numbers where the first digit is an even number. (**WHY NOT?**)

This is **ELIOT'S NUMBERS CRUNCH LAW 1**.

I simply adore experimenting with numbers and finding different laws. I've worked out lots so far and I store them all on my memory stick, which I keep with me at all times. I think I'll put them in a book when I'm 24. That's my next favourite number – at least, it *was* (you'll see why soon).

My biggest fear is of being robbed. If someone stole my memory stick with all my number laws on, I would go mad – even though I remember every detail in my brain. It would feel as if my insides had been squeezed out and trampled on by stampeding elephants. (That's called *figurative language*, but I don't use it much because I prefer more accurate stuff like precise numbers and real facts.)

Between you and me, I know exactly who'd steal my memory stick and much more, too. I'm going to tell you now about the **WORST ENEMY (TEENSY WORM)** I've ever known. He's nothing less than vile – **LIVE EVIL**. He's enough to give you **NIGHTMARES (SMEAR THING)**.

Tomorrow I will tell you the fearsome facts.

19

510

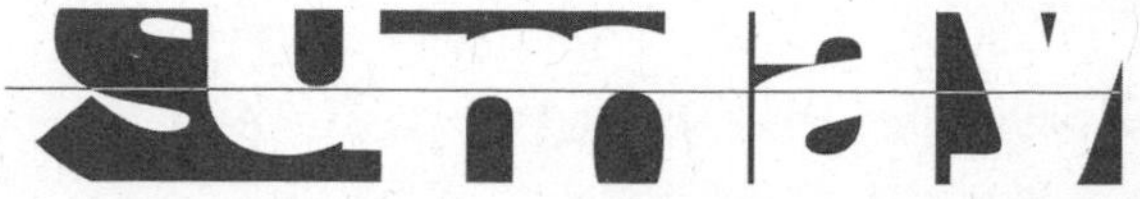

The first time I came across **VICTOR CRIDDLE (TORRID DEVIL CC)** was on the school bus on my first day at secondary school.

The **CC** of his anagram stands for Child Catcher, because that's just what he's like. He doesn't just look scary, but he traps younger kids and bullies them in all kinds of nasty ways, like offering them sweets before he thumps them.

Within days of bumping into him, I became Number 1 on his list of victims. He's two years older than me and much bigger. Here are some facts about my worst enemy in the world – the horrible, vile, repulsive Victor Criddle:

1. He lives in the next street to me. They call the Criddles 'The family from hell'.

2. He's had more fights than I've had Mrs Eve's biscuits – and that's loads.

3. He's been suspended from school more than anyone else – apart from his sister.

4. He's banned from the supermarket down the road because he weed over

the mushrooms. So I called him Victor Widdle (which I consider a good play on words). But he kicked me.

5. He stuck drawing pins in Miss Milligan's bike tyres (as well as up through her saddle), which I would think is a criminal offence, as well as being a bit painful.

So there I was, doing no harm to anyone on the school bus, when Victor Criddle came and sat next to me.

'Do yer want a sweet?' he said.

Even though he looked scary and just like the Child Catcher, I thought he was being friendly, so I said, 'Thanks very much,' and I took a *Celebrations* from the bag.

I unwrapped the mini Mars and took a bite. Yuck. It tasted dreadful and he was squawking and squealing – which is his way of laughing. My mouth was burning and I thought I was going to be sick.

He said he'd soaked the sweets in some kind of chilli oil, and he thought it was really funny. I told him what I thought of him and he thumped me in the mouth.

He said, 'No one argues with Victor Criddle. Victor by name, victor by nature.'

Then he got me in an arm lock until I couldn't breathe. Everyone else on the bus thought it was funny, but I felt like I was dying.

From then on Victor Criddle hasn't left me alone. He calls me 'Weirdo' and shouts it at me across the street, across the bus park or even in the library. He's made my life a misery.

Mr Adam said I should keep out of Victor Criddle's way and try to ignore him. I don't think that deals with the problem. I'm not really bothered about being called names – it's the other stuff that gets to me.

Before I tell you about the worst thing he did, I must mention Hannah. She's a Year 11 library prefect who understood everything about all that happened. I don't talk to girls much, but Hannah's different and she seems quite clever.

I like Hannah for three reasons:

1. **HANNAH** is a great palindrome, but her second name is so nearly one as well. Her full name is Hannah Widdows. (If it was **WODDOW** she would be perfect and I would have to marry her).

2. Hannah reads all the time and she must have read half the books in the library. She knows lots of stuff and she uses

incredible words. I'm teaching her to talk backwards.

She always puts WRM or BTW in her texts – short for 'Which Reminds Me' and 'By The Way'. It's her special thing.

3. Hannah and I often eat our sandwiches together in the library office. She's got this thing where she has to eat her food in alphabetical order, which I think is so cool. I'd love to see her eat alphabet soup. She laughs at the way I guard the library biscuit tin and she calls me Cerberus guarding the Underworld of Jammy Dodgers (whatever that means).

I can't wait till I'm in Year 11, like Hannah. She tells me some of the stuff she's done in Maths and Physics. It sounds awesome.

The other great thing about being in Year 11 is the number. Probably 11 is my third-favourite number. **ELIOT'S NUMBERS CRUNCH LAWS: LAW 2** on the next page says why.

When I'm in Year 11 I'll be sad in some ways, because Hannah will be at university and I won't have anyone to eat my sandwiches with in alphabetical order. But I'll be so happy, too. That's because Victor Criddle won't be at school anymore.

I expect he'll be in prison.

ELIOT'S NUMBERS CRUNCH LAWS: LAW 2

The number 11 is amazing.

Only two numbers in the 11 times table are not palindromes.

If you didn't know, these are the answers to 11 x 10 and 11 x 12.

Let me tell you another interesting fact about the 11 times table.

Each number, when you add their digits, goes up in a pattern:

11: 1 + 1 = 2 22: 2 + 2 = 4

33: 3 + 3 = 6 44: 4 + 4 = 8

55: 5 + 5 = 10 and so on…

Clever!

This is **ELIOT'S NUMBERS CRUNCH LAW 2**.

Eliot's 10 favourite palindromes for slipping into everyday conversation:

- **DRAB AS A FOOL, ALOOF AS A BARD**
- **DRAW PUPIL'S LIP UPWARD**
- **MURDER FOR A JAR OF RED RUM**
- **NO LEMON, NO MELON**
- **RISE TO VOTE, SIR**
- **SENILE FELINES**

- ☛ **STACK CATS**
- ☛ **STEP ON NO PETS**
- ☛ **WAS IT A CAR OR A CAT I SAW?**
- ☛ **YO, BANANA BOY!**

Can you make up some questions with these as the replies? You'll notice that I've put them in alphabetical order, because that's just what librarians do.

11

13

73

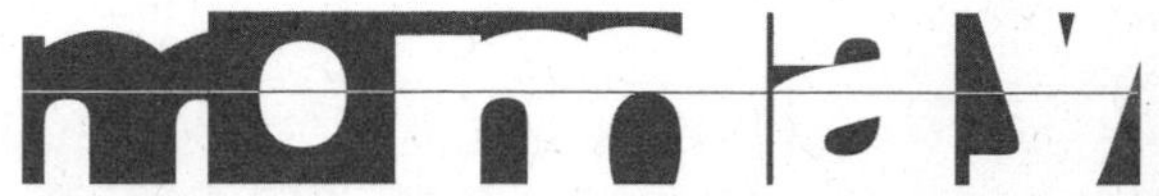

Mrs Eve told me once that she dreaded every Friday 13th. Lots of people get a bit wobbly about that day and date for some reason.

If you want to know the word for the fear of Friday 13th, it's *Paraskevidekatriaphobia* (which I think is the coolest word on the planet and could score you 44 at Scrabble even before any double letter scores).

44 is an epic Eliot number and features in Law 2. Mr Adam is 44, which is old but awesome.

Friday 13th never used to bother me, until the worst thing happened to me on that date. It was the day Victor Criddle struck like never before. It was the day that changed everything and triggered a chain of criminal events.

I will never forget it.

It was lunchtime and Mrs Eve had popped out of the library, so I was in charge. Friday is Year 11's library day, and all was fine till Victor Criddle barged in swearing and shouting at me:

'Oi, Weirdo, I want a book.'

I tried to tell him that, being Year 9, his library day was on Wednesdays, but however much I told him, he just wouldn't listen. He just got louder and swore twenty-six times.

'Shut yer face, Weirdo. I want that football book. The one about the Young Lions. Give it to me now or I'll smash yer face in.'

I told him he would have to wait until Mrs Eve came back and she would decide if he could borrow the book. He grabbed me by the throat and snarled like a bull terrier (that's a *simile*, but it's not really *hyperbole* because that's just how he was).

'What part of **NOW** don't you get?' he yelled, snatching the book off the display – the book with a footballer called Shahdan Sulaiman on the cover. Then he whacked me round the head with it.

I went all numb and couldn't see properly. He then put his horrible bent nose (just like the Child Catcher's crooked one) right up to mine and hissed with breath that smelt like blocked drains.

'If you tell anyone I've hit yer, I'll come round your house in the night, smash every window and set light to yer cat. That's a promise. I know where yer live and me and my brothers will come and sort you out if you don't do exactly what I tell yer. That little bash with a book was nothing. If you want a nose like mine, no teeth, and a metal plate in yer head, just grass on me and I'll put the boot in big time.'

Although I didn't really understand everything he said, I knew this wasn't just a threat. He meant every word of it. He and his brothers terrorised anyone who dared to upset them.

As if I needed any further warnings, he then whispered in my ear, 'If yer mum don't want her nice metallic blue Nissan dealt with, yer'd better do as yer told. Clear?'

I nodded. It was all I could do. It wasn't worth the risk of reporting him to Mrs Eve, because I knew that could make things worse. Mr Adam would just tell me to 'avoid confrontation, keep away from him and don't wind him up'.

(Anyway, how can you wind a person up if they don't wear a watch? All Victor Criddle has on his wrist is a gross tattoo.)

Just then Hannah came to my rescue and said quietly, 'Sorry, Victor – we're having a bit of trouble with the fingerprint reader at the moment so we're not able to process loans at the minute. If you pop back at the end of lunch, we'll see what we can do. I'll keep the book safe for you. How's that?'

Amazingly he didn't swear or shout. He just grabbed me by the collar and snarled again, 'OK, Weirdo. Bring that book and give it to me on the bus. If yer don't, yer dead.'

So I said, 'Do you mean to say you would commit murder for a book, Victor?'

He just grunted. 'In your case, yeah.'

I thought I would try to deflect his aggression with something verbal so I said, 'You wouldn't just be committing homicide but libricide.' (*Libri* is Latin for books).

'In your case, it'd be weirdicide. If I don't get that book for when I get home, I'll smash yer

teeth so far down yer throat that you'll need a long-handled broom to brush 'em.'

He threw me backwards onto the booking-out desk and off he stomped.

I just stared at the door after he'd gone. My tie was wrenched round my neck, I was still feeling numb from the hit on the head and I even felt a bit sick.

Hannah pushed the football book into my hand.

'I think it might be a good idea if you take this and give it to him on the bus home. Otherwise he could turn nasty.'

I was about to argue, as it seemed like I was giving in to his threats. But there again, I knew Hannah was being wise, because that's what she is.

'But we won't be able to book this out to him if we can't scan his thumbprint.'

(Extra information: We've got one of those ace systems where we don't use library tickets or cards. Each library user just presses their thumb on the scanner, which takes a reading in milliseconds and converts the image into a unique digital sequence, which is then encrypted and stored. This is called *biometrics* and I often like to examine the software that makes this work.)

Hannah looked at me with one of her funny looks – but I never know what it means.

'It *is* still working, but I said it wasn't just to get rid of him. You'll have to book it out on your thumbprint instead. It's no big deal. BTW, the only other time Victor Criddle took a book out, the scanner wouldn't work on him. WRM, he's the only one the computer didn't like. I'm not surprised, either.'

She didn't need to tell me all that, as I'd already analysed the problem.

When the thumbprint reader didn't work and Victor Criddle got all stressy, I later checked the scan with enlarged printouts of his thumbprint.

No wonder it didn't match – he'd obviously had a fight (or been bitten by his ferret), as his thumb was all scarred and scratched, so his print was no longer the same and the digital sequence didn't match up.

I flicked through the football book about the Young Lions and the footballer Shahdan Sulaiman.

'Tell you what,' I said to Hannah, 'I'll take this book out, but it's our secret. We'll call it Operation Shahdan. From now on we can refer to Victor Criddle as Shahdan – our own special codename.'

Hannah liked that idea and I put the book in my bag so I could give it to 'Shahdan' on the bus home. That was my plan – but it didn't go quite like I thought it would.

Shahdan (alias Victor Criddle) was nowhere to be seen on the school bus. Apparently he'd been caught doing something terrible in the boiler room and was on an after-school detention.

So now I had a problem. His words were still shouting inside my head: 'If I don't get that book for when I get home, I'll smash yer teeth so far down yer throat that you'll need a long-handled broom to brush 'em.'

As I hate going to the dentist at the best of times, there was only one thing for it. I would have to take that book round to Victor Criddle's house that evening if I didn't want to lose all my teeth, get beaten into a pulp or endanger Mum's car, the cat and all our windows.

Although I knew that the dreaded Criddle house was at the end of the row and next to the alley leading into the park, I wasn't prepared for the shock when I got to the front gate, with the book clutched in my hands.

There it was – the number on their door: 24. Until that moment, the number 24 had been one of my very favourites. From then on, it will never be quite the same. My **NUMBERS**

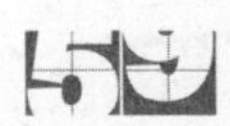

CRUNCH LAW 3 will probably end up at the bottom of my list, but here it is in case you want to know something magic about the number 24.

ELIOT'S NUMBERS CRUNCH LAWS: LAW 3

Another reason why 12 is my favourite number is because it comes between two prime numbers (11 and 13). That's rare!

(*In case you forgot: prime numbers are numbers greater than 1 that cannot be divided by any number except themselves and one.*)

The prime numbers smaller than 100 are: 2, 3, 5, 7, 11, 13, 17, 19, 23, 29, 31, 37, 41, 43, 47, 53, 59, 61, 67, 71, 73, 79, 83, 89, 97 ...

... and they go on for ever!

Nobody has yet found a pattern to predict prime numbers – but I'm working on it.

24 MAGIC

If you square **ANY** prime number bigger than 3, then subtract 1, the answer always divides by 24!

Example: $13^2 = 169$, then $169 - 1 = 168$.

Yes, $168 \div 7 = 24$.

Try it and see for yourself.

This is **ELIOT'S NUMBERS CRUNCH LAW 3**.

As I stood there at that front gate, with its broken 24 hanging off it, I suddenly heard,

'Oi, Weirdo – what do yer want?'

I looked up at a bedroom window where Victor Criddle peered down, spitting at me and grinning.

I called up to him, 'I've brought you your book.'

His horrible laugh was like nothing I've ever heard coming from a human. Before I knew it, his face had disappeared from his bedroom window and the front door was opening.

I should have walked away right then, but it was too late. The worst was about to happen ... the monster was emerging from the dangerous dragon's den.

(BTW this is not only *alliteration* but also a *metaphor,* because Victor Criddle isn't actually a dragon. He's worse.)

17

17

289

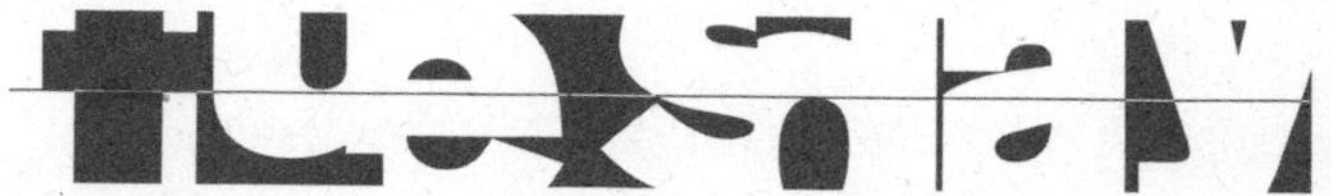

I've never liked dogs – especially big ones with hot, smelly breath.

When number 24's front door flew open and a huge Doberman leapt out in a froth of saliva and growls, I jumped back behind the front gate and slammed it shut. It didn't stop the savage beast snapping at my legs through the gaps and splattering my trousers with hot strings of slimy spit.

Above the snarls and yelps, I heard a horrible cackling howl – which was Victor Criddle's sickening laugh. He was just as scary as his pet werewolf. (I'm not sure if this is a *metaphor* or just *hyperbole*. Or maybe it's the actual truth.)

Beyond the slobbering jaws in front of me (both the dog's and 'Shadhan's'), I saw a row of hutches where ferrets were scampering up and down and squealing. The front garden (it was nothing like a proper garden – just a scrap yard) was littered with a rusty fridge, a torn leather sofa, an upside-down motorbike with a wheel missing, various exhaust pipes and three wheelie bins crammed full of junk. All buzzing with flies.

Victor Criddle pulled on the dog's collar, not to stop it chewing me to pieces, but so he could get past it to lunge at me and grab the book from my fingers.

'Leave him, Sabre. He's Weirdo. If you bite him, you'll catch something geeky and turn into a librarian.

'This is the book I want. You're not so stupid as you look, Weirdo. I thought I'd have to come round and do your place in to teach you a lesson for not doing as you were told.'

I tried to be helpful and said, 'It's due back in two weeks on the 27th, but I suggest 25th, which is your library day.'

The next thing I knew was a burning pain round my ear where he smacked the book on my head again. I nearly fell over, and as I was trying to get my balance back I heard a gruff, 'Oi, Vic – who's that kid?'

'He's a wimpy, weedy, weirdo from school. He's well odd.'

Standing at the front door was one of Victor Criddle's older brothers. I could tell he was a brother because he looked just the same, with an identical bent nose and scary eyes. He was just bigger – like a picture in a book in the library about the Yeti.

'Well tell him to hide these quick. They're coming to raid us.'

He threw two big boxes onto the ferret hutches.

'Keep these in yer shed, kid. If yer say a word, you'll wake up with stitches and bits of yer face missing.'

I could hear a police siren getting louder as the bigger Criddle rushed over to me with the boxes.

'Put your arms out and hold these.'

'What are they?' I asked.

'None of your business. They're boxes of cartons, that's all. Just get moving. Fast.'

The boxes weren't as heavy as they looked, but I was still struggling to hold them both, when suddenly the two Criddles ran indoors, dragging the barking Doberman with them. Their front door slammed shut and I was left to stagger home, struggling to peer over the top of the boxes.

I looked back to see Victor Criddle making obscene gestures at me from his bedroom window, just as a police car came squealing round the corner.

I carried on walking and as I turned into my road I looked over my shoulder to see two police cars screech to a halt outside number 24. Eight policemen ran through the gate, but I knew it wasn't a good idea to hang around and watch.

I carried on towards home and eventually stumbled my way into our back garden to put the boxes in the shed. I was just about to go indoors when I decided it might be interesting to take a look inside one of the boxes – so I did.

Both boxes held 20 cartons of cigarettes. Each carton held 10 packets. Each packet contained 20 cigarettes. So how many cigarettes in 2 boxes?

That's a lot of cigarettes to have in your shed. I looked on my laptop to find out how much a packet of cigarettes costs. This brand was £7.60 a packet, so you can work out how much these two boxes were worth.

It was only then that I realised I had just become a criminal. After all, it's a criminal offence to receive stolen goods and I had no doubt that Big Criddle had just stolen them and passed them on to me for safe-keeping.

So now I had another problem – just what should I do with thousands of stolen cigarettes? What would you have done? (BTW this is not a *rhetorical* question but one you should be able to answer for yourself.)

I didn't tell Mum what was hidden in the shed, or about what happened on my worst Friday 13th ever. She would have got really stressed and would have needed to go to the doctor again.

I decided I'd ask Hannah for advice on Monday. Now that I was a criminal I had to think like one – so I couldn't just phone, text or email her. Police forensic experts might use digital evidence to prove I was the receiver of stolen goods. From now on I would have to be really careful. I wondered what Sherlock Holmes would have done in my situation.

On Saturday morning I was woken by Mum screaming. Her car was parked outside our house and it was covered in red spray paint. Vandals had struck in the night and, of course, I knew exactly who it was. I felt really furious and frightened at the same time.

Mum was in a terrible state and she phoned the police. They told her to leave the car just where it was and an officer would call round to see the damage and fill in a form.

Mum took some tablets and went back to bed with a migraine, while I did Sudoku and watched TV. It wasn't until 17.27 that the police called. I answered the door to a WPC and I took her into the sitting room. Mum was still in bed.

'I'm going to tell you about the crime,' I began. 'I know exactly what happened and I want you to go round to number 24 Rutland Drive and arrest them. You'll need a few strong officers, as the Criddles are big and tough and they've got dogs and ferrets. I want you to lock up Victor Criddle because he's a bully and it was him who sprayed my mum's car.'

She looked at me and smiled in an odd sort of way.

'Can you prove it was him?' she asked.

I told her that that was surely *her* job and the skill of CSI officers to find all trace evidence.

'There are likely to be fibres on Mum's car that will match exactly Victor Criddle's clothes. There is bound to be paint on his clothes, too, and spray cans at his house – matching the exact paint at the crime scene. Possibly flakes of blue metallic paint from Mum's car would be under Criddle's fingernails, which chemical analysis would match up. There may even be dog hairs on the car that match his Doberman and there are likely to be fingerprints. If you need an enlarged thumbprint of his, I can provide a copy first thing on Monday morning. It's on our library system.'

She gave me another silly smile.

'It's been raining all afternoon, so the vehicle in question will be washed clean of such evidence, I'm afraid. Besides ... '

I have to admit that I shouted at her then. 'Well why didn't you come earlier, then? What's the point of investigating a crime when the crime scene has been contaminated?'

She asked me why I was so certain that it was Victor Criddle who'd vandalised the car. It was time for me to confess that I was an accomplice to theft because I was made to hide the stolen goods.

I asked her to follow me out to the shed, where she would discover all the evidence she

needed to be able to make an arrest of the Criddle gang of thieves.

I opened the shed door and pointed to the corner where I'd hidden the boxes of cigarette cartons. She smiled oddly again and just said, 'Where?'

I couldn't believe it. They'd gone.

Back in the house the policewoman told me that 'off the record' the Criddles were currently under investigation for various incidents but, due to lack of evidence, she was unable to add this case to their enquiries.

I shouted at her again, 'But Victor Criddle is **HORRIBLE**.'

She told me it was not a crime to be horrible and if it was, the prisons would be full twenty times over. She said they would give us a crime number for this case of deliberate vandalism of Mum's car and they would keep an eye on things, but there was nothing more she could do.

'But you've got to stop Victor Criddle!'

I think I must have shouted louder than ever, because Mum came downstairs looking very drowsy, just as the WPC said 'Unless any particular individual was caught in the act of vandalism or captured on CCTV, there is no

hard evidence as to who committed the offence and, even though we may suspect Victor Criddle, there are no further formal proceedings to be taken.'

After the police officer had gone, I went outside to look at Mum's car more closely. Lines and squiggles of red paint were all over the bonnet, roof and doors. It was only later when I looked at it from my bedroom window that I could make out a few letters.

It said: becos u opend the box.

Just because I'd dared to peep inside one of the boxes, they'd done that to Mum's car. I knew that it was also a warning to me to keep my mouth shut.

I went back into the shed to see if I could find just one trace of incriminating evidence to get Victor Criddle locked up for good. Nothing.

When I went to bed that night, I lay thinking for hours. Lots of questions were going through my head.

I always keep a notepad by my bed, so I can jot down special number rules, puzzles and stuff. I thought of Victor running into his house, so I made an anagram from his road name:

DEVIL TURD RAN (RUTLAND DRIVE).

Then I thought of the empty shed and wrote:

NO TRACE NOT ONE CARTON.

(*That's what I call a comic ironic palindromic chronic shame.*)

It would take a mega-crime before the police would decide to act on my advice.

The weeks that followed the Criddles' attack on Mum's car were the worst in my life. Not a day went by when Shadhan (I couldn't even say his real name) didn't torment me, threaten me, hit me, spit at me or take things from my bag. Some days he made me give him money and sandwiches.

Then the worst thing of all happened, when he gripped me in a headlock. He grabbed the cord round my neck and wrenched off my memory stick, then threw it down a drain. I was so upset that I shouted and screamed at him – but he only laughed even more. I couldn't speak for the rest of the day.

There was no point trying to tell anyone what he did because:

a) no one wanted to know,

b) it made me feel like I couldn't look after myself, so I was a useless failure, and

c) he told me what he and his brothers would do to me and my Mum if I ever told anyone.

I couldn't talk to Mum about any of this, because when she gets upset she takes even more tablets and I can't wake her up. Hannah knew about some of what was going on, but I didn't feel I could talk to her either, especially as she was in the middle of some extra exams.

No one understood how miserable I was until three things helped to cheer me up.

1) Friday 12th July arrived (my favourite date) and it was a super scorching sunny summer day. (WRM – that's alliteration

to change the mood and make things brighter.)

2) It was the day before the school fete and I was in charge of selling raffle tickets to Year 7. Mr Adam said I had to be a genius because I could remember which ticket numbers each person bought. It's just a memory trick I've got, as numbers are my thing.

3) The following week was Year 9 camp, so Victor Criddle would be away for a whole week and I would be free of his bullying.

Unfortunately, Mr Adam was also going on the camp (which is quite amazing as he's really old – at 44 – to be sleeping outside).

I don't like it when he's not at school and someone else takes our class. I like things to stay the same always and I get a bit stressy when stuff or people get changed.

Even though my whole life was pants, that Friday 12th was the start of something better.

The bus journey to school wasn't good because Shadhan Criddle was hyper, as he was going off to camp the next day. He and another boy had a bit of a fight on the back seat and Shadhan

ended up pushing a tissue up his nose to stop a nosebleed.

As I hadn't had any breakfast, I took from my bag a nice red shiny apple to munch. But before I could take a bite, he whipped it from my hand and sunk his teeth into it. He cackled and scoffed the lot. Then, as always, he rummaged through my bag and took a Mars Bar.

There was lots going on that day and Mrs Harris looked in a bit of a fluster when I went to her office at morning break. Her desk was piled with money bags and bundles of twenty pound notes.

'Hello Eliot,' she squeaked. 'Don't tell me you've got more money for me! I've got so much here, what with the raffle money, camp payments and everything else, I could run away and go on a world cruise.'

She gave one of her silly giggles.

'But wouldn't that be stealing, Mrs Harris?' I said.

'Yes, Eliot, it most certainly would. It was a joke, poppet. Now, how much money do you need to hand in?'

I told her I had sold two hundred and forty raffle tickets, so I had £120 to hand in – but she

didn't need to count the money as I had already checked it.

'It's just as well you're such an honest and reliable boy, Eliot,' she said. 'I wish more people were like you.'

'There's something special I must show you,' I told her.

I was really excited about a particular twenty pound note because I always look at the serial numbers on banknotes, as they can be quite interesting. It's very rare to see a palindromic number on a twenty pound note, so I was delighted to see this one: **EE33 876678**.

I told Mrs Harris that this was a particularly fascinating number for all sorts of reasons. One of them was the sum total of all the digits, which is one of those numbers I really love (for a start, it's the smallest number with 10 factors, which I find big-time mega awesome).

Anyway, I'd already explained this to Mr Adam and Mrs Eve and shown them the twenty pound note. Miss Milligan in the next office said she ought to keep it, because it was only one number different from her phone number. I told her that was truly cosmic and I was ecstatic.

She just said, 'That's nice dear,' and smiled weirdly.

I left Mrs Harris surrounded by all that money and I went to the library, as I had an important job to do. I remember the time then was 10.56, so there were fourteen minutes of break-time left. This was information that would later be of use in constructing a timeline of events.

I went back to see Mrs Harris at lunchtime to ask her how much money the raffle had collected so far, but I heard her before I got to the door. It wasn't her silly giggle this time but it sounded like she was crying.

Miss Milligan saw me at the door and said, 'Not now, Eliot. We're sorting out a problem.'

'Can I help?' I said, looking into the office, where I could see the safe was open.

'Thank you, Eliot, but this is a matter for the police. There's been a burglary in here, I'm afraid.'

I took out my phone. 'In that case, you can use my camera if you like. You ought to take a photo of the crime scene and you must make sure you don't touch or move anything. Shall I take a picture for you?'

She didn't say anything because she went to give Mrs Harris another tissue – so I just pointed my camera and clicked.

They were too concerned about whatever had happened to bother with me, so I went to the library to upload my crime-scene image on the computer. I could soon see all sorts of interesting clues, so I was ready if the police wanted my advice. Sherlock Holmes would have solved this in minutes.

Instead of form-time at the end of the afternoon, the whole school had to go into the sports hall for a special assembly. A man in a stripy suit and a yellow tie stood at the front, with two policemen just behind him.

'Some of you may have heard,' he began, 'that a burglary has occurred on these school premises. A substantial amount of money has been stolen

and this is a very serious matter. I am in charge of the investigation and I need your help. The thief or thieves, whoever he, she or they happen to be, struck in broad daylight, so there are bound to be witnesses amongst you in here. Indeed, the culprit may also be sitting in front of me right now.

'We are already pursuing various lines of enquiry and it will only be a matter of time before we shall be making an arrest. We are asking for your cooperation, particularly as it is your money, stolen from your school. We shall be searching all bags as a routine procedure as you leave school this afternoon.

'I want you all to reflect over this weekend and ask yourself two questions. First, have you seen anything or anyone suspicious today? Anything at all.

'Second, if you happen to hear or know any information about this crime – or indeed, if you were part of it – I would like to hear from you. If anyone's conscience is telling them to speak to one of our officers in confidence, I would urge you to tell us as soon as possible.'

Everyone was talking about the burglary on the bus home. Thankfully, as Year 9 were going off to camp early next morning, a certain person

was in an unusually good mood and giving everyone sweets.

Someone asked him how much money he was taking to camp and he shouted for all to hear, 'Millions 'cos I'm loaded.' He took a twenty pound note from inside his sock and waved it in the air.

I sat quietly and tidied my bag, as the police had gone through it and left it in a mess. Then I sat back and looked out of the bus window all the way home. It gave me important time to think and plan my letter. I was going to write to the police to tell them about all the clues I had seen and other likely evidence. But most of all, I had to tell them the name they needed to know.

This is a copy of the letter I later printed and sent to the police. It took me ages to write because of all the long words (to make it the sort of letter Sherlock Holmes would send).

Dear Criminal Investigation Department,

This is an anonymous letter because if the person I am about to name ever discovers I have written it, I will be at serious risk of major violence.

I have examined the evidence relating to the theft of thousands of pounds in cash from the safe in Castle Priory School's finance office. There can be no doubt that the criminal you must arrest is a Year 9 boy by the name of Victor Criddle. The evidence from the crime scene is as follows.

1) *Fingerprints. Victor Criddle's fingerprints are likely to be on items on the office desk, but also inside the safe itself. Try looking on some of the empty plastic money bags he left behind.*

2) *DNA. Victor Criddle's blood is probably on a discarded tissue in the corner of the office. If so, this would place him at the crime scene on the day of the theft.*

3) *DNA and/or dental impression. If you examine the apple core under the desk at the crime scene, you may obtain the criminal's DNA from traces of saliva, as well as teeth marks that will probably match the dental records of Victor Criddle.*

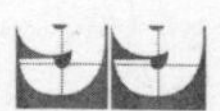

4) *A faint purple shoeprint on a carpet tile just inside the office door is likely to match exactly the pattern on Victor Criddle's shoe. As you know, all shoeprints are unique.*

There will also be two other pieces of incriminating evidence:

a) *The crime, as you have probably already calculated, must have taken place between 11.10 and 11.35, while the finance office was left unattended. If you examine CCTV images between those times from the camera at the reception area, you will see that Victor Criddle was out of his lesson and in close proximity to the crime scene at*

the exact time of the crime. This must make him a prime suspect.

b) I would advise you to examine Victor Criddle's bedroom at 24 Rutland Drive, where you are bound to find indisputable evidence linking him to the crime. Your searches at school did not find the stolen money in his bag because he hid it inside his clothes.

I trust this gives you enough information to make a speedy arrest and to lock away Victor Criddle for a very long time.

Yours faithfully,

An Amateur Detective (similar to Sherlock Holmes)

100

24

12

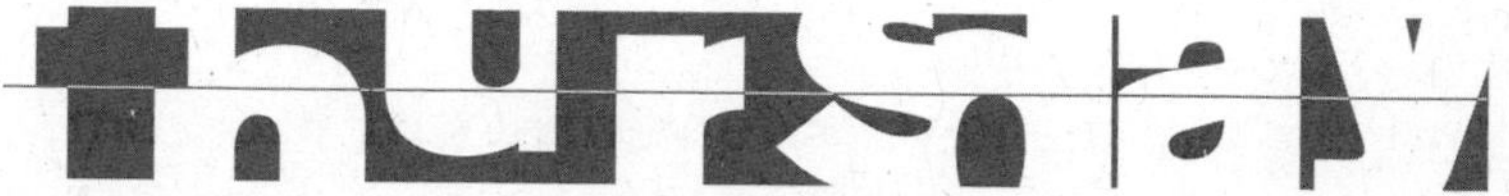

News of the burglary was in all the papers. It was reported as the worst crime ever to hit our school, with over two hundred twenty pound notes being stolen. Everyone at school was talking about it.

The following Monday evening I saw two police cars outside Victor Criddle's house at number 24. Within a few hours he had been arrested. A police car apparently collected him

from the campsite and took him off for questioning.

They say the police found some of the stolen money and the key to the school safe in Victor Criddle's bedroom. By the end of the week he was charged with theft and everyone was saying that he'll be sent away.

YES!!!

Since hearing that news my life has never been better.

So what do you think of my Sherlock Holmes skills? You may think the police didn't need my help at all. Even so, you have to admit that the result was just what I wanted. It was perfect, especially as (now brace yourself for a bit of a surprise) Victor Criddle was totally innocent, for once.

Honestly – he didn't do it. Only ***I*** know who did.

Can you work out who *really* committed the crime?

Before I tell you, you ought to stop reading on and think about the evidence for a while.

Try a bit of detective work of your own. Who do *you* think the thief was?

One of the people I've already told you about was the real burglar, but only I know who it was.

The answer to who stole all the money is hidden in this blog. Their name is in my NUMBERS CRUNCH LAW 2. So go back and take a look. It's on page 43.

Look at the first capital letter of each sentence in LAW 2 and see what they spell backwards. It's the name of the burglar.

Are you shocked?

Just in case you need a second clue, see if you can make a four–word sentence from **HE TIME FAITH**. Or if you prefer it in just three words **AIM WEST**.

Hannah sent me a text: Up locked him get to Shahdan frame as well as crime the commit to you of clever was it.

She's started sending texts backwards. Even so, I've deleted it, as well as her final anagram: **MEET RICH PREFECT**.

Maybe I need to explain a bit more, in case you are still a bit puzzled. The last part of my

blog will make it all clear ... before I wipe everything clean forever.

I'd planned it for ages. The day was perfect. I sent Mrs Gibson (my Maths teacher) an email from Mrs Eve's computer at morning break: *'Please can Eliot come to the library for 5 minutes straight away? Thanks.'*

I was let out of the classroom at 11.14 and I went straight to the library to collect a carrier bag I'd hidden behind the shelf marked CRIME. I took it to the finance office, making sure I avoided all CCTV cameras on the way.

Mrs Harris had just left her office for the usual finance meeting, so I quickly nipped in, took the safe key from the purse in her handbag, opened the safe and stuffed all the banknotes from inside into my carrier bag, after removing my items in it.

I carefully left those bits of evidence at the scene, apart from a bottle of Ribena, from which I poured a trickle onto the floor outside the door. I did all this in 29.4 seconds and I quickly left, passing Victor Criddle in the corridor.

I'd also sent an email from Mrs Eve's computer to his teacher, asking for him to go to the finance office for an urgent message and to come

through the main entrance. (All emails I've since deleted.)

Criddle evidently walked into the finance office just as I planned, treading the Ribena into the carpet tiles and leaving his shoeprint. **PERFECT**.

There were a few items in my school bag that Victor Criddle had rummaged through on the bus that morning, in his usual search for money or food. His fingerprints were all over them, but mine weren't. So, using rubber gloves, I'd placed the roll of Sellotape from my bag onto Mrs Harris's desk, as well as a Pritt Stick (with a perfect thumbprint on it). A plastic money bag

he'd taken a pound from also had his fingerprints all over it, so I put that inside the safe.

When he'd got off the bus that morning, Victor Criddle had thrown two things at me. One was the tissue he'd used for his nosebleed and the other was the core of my apple he'd just eaten. I'd kept them both, then simply dropped one in the corner of the office and the other under the desk.

My real stroke of genius was planting evidence in his bedroom. It was Hannah who gave me the idea. It wasn't anything she said: just her name. What do you get from an anagram of **HANNAH WIDDOWS**?

On Saturday night at two in the morning, I crept out of bed, got dressed and sneaked downstairs. Mum was fast asleep, having taken her usual tablets.

I took from the ice compartment in the fridge a special ice cube (bigger than average) that I'd made before bedtime. It had a rolled-up twenty pound note frozen inside. It was the twenty pound note with the serial number **EE33 876678** that I'd deliberately shown to many people. They all knew it was one of the banknotes that had been locked inside the safe.

With that ice cube beginning to melt in my gloved hand, I walked out into the night and went to number 24 Rutland Drive – the dreaded

Criddle house. Everything was very quiet and, just as I expected on such a warm night, all the upstairs windows were open. I gently pushed open the front gate and crept up the path to stand beneath Shahdan's empty bedroom.

While he was sleeping in a tent at camp, somewhere beneath the stars, I was taking careful aim at his open window. The ice cube flew through the air and disappeared into his room with the faintest plonk. A dog howled somewhere at the back of the house, so I quickly hurled a second missile: the key from the school safe. It landed inside without a sound and I ran.

By the time the police would search his room, the ice would have melted and evaporated,

leaving the incriminating banknote near the stolen key somewhere in the suspect's bedroom. **PERFECT**.

I turned to look back at the bedroom window. All was still and the dog was silent again. I smiled as I headed for home, with that unquestionable evidence waiting to be discovered inside the **SHAHDAN WINDOW** (the answer to the last anagram, if you hadn't worked it out).

When I got home, I went into our back garden, took a box of matches and some scrunched-up newspaper from the shed and lit a fire on the path.

I removed the rubber gloves from my hands (the same gloves I'd used at the crime scene at school to ensure none of my fingerprints were anywhere to be found) and I threw them into the flame from the flaring newspaper. The gloves melted, bubbled, sizzled and dribbled before being engulfed in purple flames. Soon they were gone – nothing left. Just the perfect anagram:

ELIOT'S NUMBERS CRUNCH LAWS

which equals

STOLEN CASH WRM I BURN CLUES.

BTW, I wrote a letter to Victor (care of the police). The numbers down the side are important but he's not clever enough to work it out. He'll just think someone is trying to be helpful. (I didn't sign it, but he may guess it's me.)

All letters sent to suspects must get checked by officers who are trained in deciphering puzzles. That's a job I'd like one day. So here's the letter I sent to Victor – although it's really meant for the police to use in court. Then the judge will understand just what Victor is really like.

LETTER OF SUPPORT

1 *Victor Criddle doesn't bother kids much as he's usually too busy*

2 *making them laugh with his funny jokes. In fact, he's never really*

3 *bullying me or causing me real grief, and he thinks nothing of*

4 *being friendly to everyone. People respect his family, who never like*

5 *upsetting the neighbours or making big trouble. He goes on the streets*

6 *trying to stop other kids from getting into serious crime, such as*

7 *stealing, vandalising, joy-riding or getting into violent fights.*

8 *I was horrified when Victor was arrested, which must be a mistake.*

9 *Victor Criddle needs quick justice as I believe he should always be kept*

10 *on the 'Innocent' list. I will put up 'Free Victor' posters in shops, pubs and*

11 *behind bars. In fact, I would go as far as to plead with you that Victor is*

12 released immediately and given a full
pardon. I hope my proposal will be

13 seriously dealt with as soon as possible.
Thank you for reading this so carefully.

Yours faithfully,
Never Even But Odd

Can you see what I've done? They'll find my *real* message hidden inside the letter by taking only the lines with odd numbers and joining them together.

Clever, don't you think? As I said, *Never Even But Odd*. I bet Sherlock Holmes would be mega impressed.

Not usable for today only

Ground-breaking news!

Victor Criddle obviously pleaded 'not guilty'. Despite madly protesting his innocence, he's just been found guilty of the burglary in court. Yay!

He'll be sent away to a kind of juvenile institution and both Mum and I have been so much happier since hearing the news. She just smiled for the first time in ages. At last.

If you ask me, I think Victor Criddle deserves what happened, after getting away with so much for so long. I just call it revenge. He always called me **ODD** – now we're **EVEN**!

As for the stolen money – it all went to charity. A children's charity, actually – for young victims of bullying, abuse and despair.

Does that make my secret and what I did right? What do you think? What would you have done in my shoes? (Which is a daft saying because my shoes probably wouldn't fit you, as I take an extra-wide fitting).

I think I know the question you still want answered. Why didn't the police find the stolen money in my bag on the afternoon of the crime, when everyone was searched?

Simple – I hid it. Where? The safest place of all ... in school, under their noses. In fact, under the custard creams inside Mrs Eve's Chamber of Secrets. No one would dare to look inside the librarian's sacred biscuit tin – or suspect its **ANOINTED GUARDIAN**. A cunning plan, don't you think?

If anyone ever asks if you know who the real thief was, **DON'T NOD**. In fact, don't say a word. It's our secret. I wrote it all down in a temporary blog because I was so proud of myself

for once ... but now I'm going to delete the lot, so that all evidence will disappear forever.

All my words will be **ERADICATED ON** – or to use the perfect anagram: **NO IDEA TRACED**. I can even sum it up with four more: **A DARE NOTICED** ... **REDO NICE DATA** ... **REACTION DEAD** ... **ACE TIN ADORED**.

—

Just right. Spot on. Job done.

BTW: The last puzzle I leave with you is this: who was the victim and who was the victor in all of this? So much for Victor getting the better of Eliot. Just who's the real *Victor* now?

BTW: I bet you can't guess why I chose the picture on the cover of this book. Any idea?

It's an anagram, of course. **ELIOT'S SECRET** = **LET'S STORE ICE**.

Magic!

alliteration

the repetition of a particular sound in the first syllables of a series of words or phrases – as in 'dangerous dragon's den'.

anagram

rearranging the letters of a word or phrase to make another word or phrase. So for example **EVIL** *is an anagram of* **VILE**.

biometrics

*refers to the identification of humans by their (**bio**logical) characteristics, such as a fingerprint or retina scan. It's often used as a way of controlling access to places.*

enigma

a person, a thing or an event that is puzzling or hard to explain.

figurative language

using words to describe something in a way that goes beyond their ordinary meaning. It can include, but isn't limited to, hyperbole, similes and metaphors.

hyperbole

exaggerating something to make a point (for example 'I'm so tired I could sleep for a year').

irony

saying something when it is obvious that you mean the opposite – for example 'Oh great! My watch has broken'.

metaphor

comparing two different things that are not alike, but which nevertheless have something in common. For example, 'Life is a rollercoaster'.

palindrome

a word or phrase that reads the same in either direction. For example, **NEVER ODD OR EVEN**.

paraskevidekatriaphobia

a fear of the day/date Friday 13th.

prime number

a whole number greater than 1 that can only be divided by 1 and itself (giving a whole-number answer). Thirteen is an example of prime number – as it can only be divided by itself and 1.

rhetorical question

a figure of speech where a question is asked, but the person is asking the question to make a point, without expecting an answer. For example 'Are you crazy?'.

simile

a figure of speech comparing two different things, using a word such as 'like' or 'as'. For example: 'He is sleeping like a log'.

COLD FUSION

'*A library is like a giant freezer; chock-full of delicious ideas just waiting to be thawed, fused and consumed. Each book is a frozen feast, ready to be opened and melted in the mind. Sometimes a single sentence, like a cube of ice, slides off the page ... trickling truth or seeping some chilling secret.*'

Mrs Eve, school librarian

John Townsend was born in Chelmsford, Essex, and discovered his enchantment with books at an early age. As a child, he wrote mini-dramas, silly poems and stories to tell the cat. Whether or not the cat wanted to hear them is another matter!

His love of hiking and the outdoors led him to become a geography teacher in Gloucestershire, writing pantomimes and plays for the annual drama productions. His first publication was inspired by his rusty old Morris Minor and, 200 books later, he is now a full-time writer.

www.johntownsend.co.uk

12 more reasons why 12 is so special

1. There are 12 hours in a day.
2. There are 12 months in a year.
3. There are 12 inches in a foot.
4. There are 12 signs of the Zodiac.
5. In English, twelve is the largest number that has just one syllable.
6. There are 12 pairs of ribs in the human body – unless Criddle's been at you.
7. 12 men have walked on the Moon's surface – so far.
8. There are 12 stars on the flag of Europe.
9. In British law, when you reach the age of 12 you can buy a pet (but sadly not a tiger).

10. In Britain, when you reach 12, you can legally watch a 12-certificate film.
11. 12 o'clock is midday, which is **NOON** (an ace palindrome)
12 A 12-sided shape is a **DODECAGON** (which is a cool anagram of **GONAD CODE**!) Any solid shape with twelve flat faces is a **DODECAHEDRON** (**HOODED DANCER**), which has 12 letters. That's so mega-magic!

12345678910111213141516171819202122232425262
2829303132333435363738394041424344454647484
0515253545556575859606162636465666768697071
7374757677787980818283848586878889909192939
596979899100101102103104105106107108109110
121131141151161171181191201211221231241251261
71281291301311321331341351361371381391401411
21431441451461471481491501511521531541551561
71581591601611621631641651661671681691701711
21731741751761771781791801811821831841851861
71881891901911921931941951961971981992002012
22032042052062072082092102112122132142152162
72182192202212222232242252262272282292302312
22332342352362372382392402412422432442452462
72482492502512522532542552562572582592602612
22632642652662672682692702712722732742752762
72782792802812822832842852862872882892902912
22932942952962972982993003013023033043053063
73083093103113123133143153163173183193203213
23233243253263273283293303313323333343353363
73383393403413423433443453463473483493503513
23533543553563573583593603613623633643653663
73683693703713723733743753763773783793803813
23833843853863873883893903913923933943953963
7398 04114
2413 4264
7428 4414
2443 4564
7458 4714
24734744754764774784794804814824834844854864
74884894904914924934944954964974984995005015
25035045055065075085095105115125135145155165

COLD
Fusion

Cold Fusion is a new series for readers who are curious, who enjoy a challenge and who like thinking outside the box.